I Didn't Do It

by Patricia MacLachlan and Emily MacLachlan Charest

illustrated by Katy Schneider

KATHERINE TEGEN BOOKS
An Imprint of HarperCollins Publishers

For Owen, who was the perfect puppy,
and for Tess, who is good enough
—E.C.

And for Tanga, who was
the perfect friend
—P.M.

For Dave with love,
and for Carol, in loving memory
—K.S.

Shhh . . . I'm Here

Shhh . . .
I'm here,
Born in the soft overcoat quiet of someone's closet.
With brothers and sisters
So like me
I can't tell where I end
And they begin.

Shhh . . .
Please close the door,
Turn off the light.
I'm tired.
Being born
Is
Very
Hard
Work.

Shhh . . .
Shhh . . .

No Name

Look at me!

No name yet.

Fluffy?

> **I don't like it.**

Spot?

> **No spots on me.**

Rex?

> **No.**

Rover?

> **No.**

Jack?

> **No.**

Roy?

> **No!**

> **And no**
> Bitsy
> Riley
> Fabio
> Percy
> Trace
> Or
> Willie Mo.

> **No!**

I want to be called

Big Bad Bob!

Rules

No lick!
No bite!
No jump.
No bark.
No fun.

Sit!
Stay!
Down!

I don't like your rules.

Here are **my** rules:

Eat all you want.
Sleep when you want—
 On the couch
 On the bed
 On your silk pillow.
Drooling is good.

Run off when you want—
 Across the street
 Through the garden is fine.

Get muddy.
Be happy.
Howl!

What I Don't Like

I **don't like** it when you go away.
 Where are you going??
 When are you coming back??
I **don't like** thunder.
 Loud
 I shake.
The nail clippers
 I **don't like** my feet touched.
The vacuum cleaner
 I'm leaving.
My food
 I like yours better.
The mailman
 Every single day he comes!
The baby crying
 Why does she do that?
The bath
 I **don't** need one.

Most of all I **don't like** it when you catch me
 Stealing food off the table.
Three times this week I did it,
Caught once
Didn't like it.

What I Like

Round I like
balls
balloons
bubbles
An orange
I hid somewhere.

Sweet I like
jelly beans
cookies
cake crumbs
Ice cream
Dripped from a cone.
Gum when I find it on the
sidewalk!

Water in summer I like

drinking it

swimming in it

shaking it all over.

no, not my bath.

Warm in winter I like

my fleece coat

my blanket

a winter fire.

Your lap.

I Didn't Do It

I didn't do it.

Uh-uh.

I didn't chew your slipper.

I don't like the taste of wool.

I didn't do it.

I didn't eat the buttons off your coat.

It was a bird

Flew in the window

A big bird.

It pecked the buttons off and flew away again.

I didn't do it.

I didn't eat your food.

It was the cat

Who jumped up on the table and dragged your pork

chop off.

I watched.

But it wasn't me.

I didn't do it.

I didn't bury my bone in the garden
Under your peony bush.
It was another dog—
   The hound from down the street
   His name is Rascal, I think.

Not *me*.
Not *me*.
Not *me*.

I didn't do it.
I didn't bury my bone in the garden

Rain

I like rain.
Things stick to me
  Like dirt
   And leaves
   And grass.

I like rain.
When I come inside
I like to pull your nice wool sweater
  Off the bed
   And roll in it.
I can dry myself.
I don't have to bother you!

You'll be proud when you see it
On the floor.
Good puppy, you'll say!

Right?

What Did I Do??

What did I do?

You don't like my present to you?

I went outside and caught it myself—

I went down a hole—

Look!

  All furry brown and white

  It's too little to be scary.

Wait! Where are you going?

Come back!

Look.

It is still alive!

It just hopped under your bed.

What did I do?

You don't like my present to you?

Big

Big paws
Giant
Big legs
Trees
Big tail
Sweep, sweep
Big puff puppy.

I flop
I gallop
I tumble
I fall.

I fill up the couch
I fill up the room
I fill up the car
I fill the sky!

Some people think I am too big.
Too clumsy
But not you.
   You love my paws.
   You love my legs.
   You love my tail.

You love me **big**.

Pretty Puppy

Pretty puppy
Pretty ears
Pretty eyes
Pretty **big**
White
Teeth.

The pretty puppy touches noses with me.
The pretty puppy barks when I bark.
  At the same time
  The same way
  How can that be?
The pretty puppy wags his tail when I wag mine.
  Up
  Down
  Wag in a circle!

The pretty puppy's ears flop like mine.
The pretty puppy's tongue has a spot.
  Just
  Like
  Mine!

When I go away and come back?
Guess who's there **again?**

She Flies

She flies!

She's a puppy
But she can fly.

I fly, too.
Through the brook
Past the cows
Up, up, over the fence
Through the woods
Through the mud
Through the barn
And out again.

Hay sticks to her coat
And mine.
We race.
We run.

We fly!

One Thing, One Time

I'm perfect.

I know because they tell me so.

I *never* go to the bathroom in the house

  On the rugs

  Or bedspread

  Or on your plants.

never chew up shoes

Or the legs of fine chairs

Or your favorite scarf with the pictures of fruits

  that look so real I can smell them.

I only chewed **one thing, one time.**

Can't remember what it was.

They've forgotten.

I'm perfect.

Puppy Dreams

I can sleep
  in your hat.
I can sleep
  on the purple velvet pillow on your chair.
I can sleep
  in the cat's bed
  (if she'd ever let me)

You can carry me
  in your arms
  in your pocketbook
  in your backpack
When we go out.

But not for long.
I dreamed last night
That I was grown.
I was too big for
  your hat
  the purple velvet pillow
  the cat's bed (when she lets me)
  your arms
  your pocketbook
  your backpack.

When I am grown

I will keep you safe the way you keep me safe now.

I will keep you safe

  from winds

  and hail

  and snow.

When I am grown

I will keep watch

Over you.

Every Night

Every night you sing the song
 About the stars
 And moon.

Every night you pat my head.

Every night I climb under your quilt
And crawl

Down

Down

Down

By your warm feet.

And close my eyes.

And sleep.

Every night.